Daphne the Blind Dog

By Dawn M. Gibbons
Illustrations by Chad Thompson

With thanks to Sit Happens!
Companion Dog Training School in
Calgary, Alberta. A special thank you
to Daphne's instructor Colleen Herring
for her patience and ability to adapt
activities to be achievable for an
anxious little blind dog.

Daphne was bored. She had nothing to do. She had been adopted and now owned toys for the first time. But Daphne was blind. She couldn't see the toys and didn't know how to play with them.

"I know!" said her best friend, Dawn. "I'll take you to dog training school. They'll teach you how to use your nose to play and have fun."

On the first day of school, Dawn watched as other dogs each had a turn in the nose work class. They quickly found treats hidden in cardboard boxes and they were happy dogs.

Dawn noticed something. Even the dogs who could see used their noses for the game.

When Daphne entered the room for her turn, she could smell that other dogs had been there! She was the only dog in the room, but so many different scents made her nervous. She stood on the mat and shook with fear.

Daphne couldn't see the small boxes scattered around the room, but she could smell them. Suddenly, she smelled cheese! It was her favourite treat, but she was too frightened to try to find it. Daphne didn't understand that it was a game she could play. She stayed frozen on the mat. Dawn picked her up, hugged her, and said "It's okay, Daphne."

The dogs took turns playing the game. On Daphne's final try, she was still too scared to walk farther into the room. The teacher put a piece of cheese near the edge of the mat. When Daphne smelled it, she couldn't resist anymore. She took a tiny step, stretched her neck, and finally ate her treat. "Good for you, Daphne! I'm proud of you!" Dawn said.

Almost every day, Dawn hid treats in boxes for Daphne to practise the game at home. In her own house, Daphne was more relaxed, so it was easier to focus. She quickly learned to use her nose to find which boxes had the treats.

On the next school day, Daphne felt a little braver and was willing to leave the mat. The teacher put some boxes close to Daphne. She sniffed and sniffed like she had practised at home. She smelled chicken! Each time she found a treat inside a box, Daphne enjoyed her tasty snack!

By the third class, Daphne really understood the game. Although she moved more slowly than the other dogs, she did the nose work very well. Daphne was able to find the boxes with treats every time.

For the next three classes, the other dogs were in a second room. They were ready for the challenge of searching for treats hidden in objects with a different smell than cardboard boxes—like plastic toys and wicker baskets.

Daphne needed more practice, so she stayed in the first room where new dogs were just starting school. The teacher helped Daphne by always keeping the boxes in a smaller area for her. Daphne confidently found her treats. She used her nose as well as the other dogs.

After a few classes, it was time for the new group of dogs to play the game in the second room. This time, Daphne was ready for the challenge. She found treats in a metal toy truck, a plastic pail, and even an empty paper towel roll.

Eventually, Daphne had nose work classes outside. The teacher used peanut butter to stick pieces of meat to a large parked car—low enough for Daphne to reach. The game was trickier now! There were so many more distractions outside! Daphne could smell the grass and the animals that had walked on it. She could hear birds, cars, and planes. It took a moment for Daphne to focus with her nose. When she did, she found her treats and happily licked them off the car.

On the last day of school, the teacher hid treats in plastic eggs and tossed them on the grass. Daphne picked up the scent through a very tiny hole and found which of the eggs had treats. "You did it, Daphne! I'm so proud of you!" Dawn said.

At home, Daphne had lots to do. She really liked to play the sniffing game from school. By using her nose, she also learned to roll a new ball that dropped treats for her.

Daphne had fun playing and had more confidence than ever before. Dawn even taught her some tricks. She learned to sit, lie down, and lift her paw. Standing on her hind legs was her favourite trick of all! Daphne wasn't bored anymore.